SIMON & SCHUSTER BOOKS FOR YOUNG READERS

An imprint of Simon & Schuster Children's Publishing Division

1230 Avenue of the Americas, New York, New York 10020

Text copyright © 1995 by Margaret Mayo

Illustrations copyright © 1995 by Louise Brierley

Originally published in Great Britain by Orchard Books, 1995

First American Edition, 1996

All rights reserved including the right of reproduction in whole or in part in any form.

SIMON & SCHUSTER BOOKS FOR YOUNG READERS is a trademark of Simon & Schuster.

The text of this book is set in Perpetua.

The illustrations are rendered in watercolors.

Printed and bound in Singapore

First Edition

2 4 6 8 10 9 7 5 3 1

Library of Congress Cataloging-in-Publication Data

Mayo, Margaret.

[Orchard book of creation stories]

When the world was young: creation and pourquoi tales / retold by Margaret Mayo; illustrated by Louise Brierley

1st American ed.

p.   cm.

"Originally published in Great Britain by Orchard Books, 1995"—T.p. verso.

Contents: The girl who did some baking—Catch it and run!—Maui and his thousand tricks—Tortoise's big idea—Raven and the pea-pod man—Emu and Eagle's great quarrel—The magic millstones—The mud on turtle's back—Ra, the shining sun god—Feathered Snake and Huracan—Something about the stories.

1. Tales. [1. Folklore.] I. Brierley, Louise, ill. II. Title.

PZ8.1.M4627Wh   1996   398.2—dc20   95-435355   CIP   AC

ISBN: 0-689-80867-4

When the World Was Young

CREATION *and* POURQUOI *Tales*

About Creation and Pourquoi Tales

The lovely French word *pourquoi* means "why," and a *pourquoi story* is one that tries to explain just why some natural object, phenomenon, or living thing looks or behaves the way it does. Some *pourquoi* stories answer more than one question. In *Catch it and Run!*, for instance, besides finding out how and why fire was hidden in trees, we also find out why squirrel has a curled-up tail and frog has no tail at all.

Nearly every culture has made up stories that try to answer some of the big questions we ourselves still ask. Where did people come from? How and why did we find ourselves here on this wonderful earth? And how were the earth, the sun, the moon and stars, and all other living things made? We call the stories that try to answer these really big questions *creation stories*. Usually there is a god or a powerful mysterious being, like Raven, in charge, making decisions and doing things. BUT—look out—tucked inside some creation stories you will discover neat little *pourquoi* tales, explaining why monkeys look like people, or why the Australian kookaburra laughs at dawn—that sort of thing!

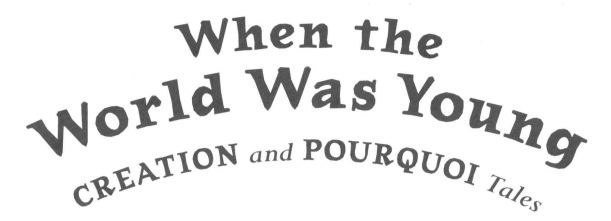

When the World Was Young

CREATION and POURQUOI Tales

retold by
MARGARET MAYO

illustrated by
LOUISE BRIERLEY

Simon & Schuster Books for Young Readers

Contents

★

for A.L.C.
L.B.

for Ursula Sewart
M.M.

The Girl who did Some Baking

Have you ever wondered why children come in all sorts of different colors? Well, have you? It's because of something that happened long ago.

In that far-off time, there was no earth and it was always dark. But high above the black night sky, in a place that was full of light, lived Nyame, the Sky God. And inside Nyame there lived some spirit people.

Now Nyame liked making things, and a time came when he decided to make something very special. First he took an enormous basket and filled it with earth and planted it with every kind of wonderful plant. But that was not enough for Nyame. He then made lots of splendid animals and birds and insects, and set them among the plants.

11

When he had finished, Nyame stood back and admired his earth basket. "That's certainly something special!" he said. "And I know exactly where I'm going to put it!"

He carefully cut a round hole in the sky, and then he made a trapdoor that fitted the hole. He opened the trapdoor. He tied a rainbow rope to the basket and lowered it through the hole, down and down, until it reached the place where the earth basket is today.

Light flooded through the hole and lit up everything below—and that hole is the round sun, which still lights up the earth when Nyame's trapdoor is open.

Nyame was pleased with his work and he admired it some more. But after a while he closed the trapdoor, and immediately it was black night down on the earth basket. "Oh, my poor animals!" said Nyame. "I had forgotten about them! They will be so frightened in the dark!"

There and then, he cut some extra holes in the sky— and those holes are the moon and stars, which still shine when Nyame's trapdoor is shut.

Nyame was fond of his earth basket, and he was constantly opening the trapdoor and looking down. Sometimes one or two of the spirit people who lived inside him would climb up into his mouth, and then they would look down as well.

One day, when Nyame was admiring his earth basket, he noticed a bare patch where nothing was growing. "I must fill that up!" he said.

So he took a small basket, the same size as the empty space, and he filled it with plants. He tied a rainbow rope to

the basket and then began to lower it through the hole in the sky.

Now one of the girl spirits who lived inside Nyame was called Iyaloda. She was lively and interested in just about everything. As soon as she heard that Nyame was lowering a small basket, she said to the boy spirit who was her special friend, "Let's go and have a look!"

"Hmmm . . . all right," he said. And, hand in hand, they crept up inside Nyame.

When they came to his mouth, Iyaloda and the boy spirit tiptoed over his tongue, up to his teeth, and leaned out over his big lips. And the next moment Nyame *sneezed!* Iyaloda and the boy spirit were whirled out of his mouth, down through the hole, and plump into the middle of the small basket.

By the time they had got their breath back, the small basket had landed and somehow fitted itself into the empty space in the earth basket.

"That was a bit unexpected," said Iyaloda. "But now that we are here, let's look around."

The two of them set off, hand in hand. At first they were quite happy. There were so many wonderful things to see. But it was not long before they began to wonder how they could get back to their home inside Nyame. They thought and thought, but they could not think of a way to reach the trapdoor up in the sky. And then they felt sad.

When darkness came, and the moon and stars began to shine, they made a shelter with some branches, curled up close to one another, and fell asleep.

As the days went by, Iyaloda and the boy spirit often felt real, deep-down sad. It was lonely living by themselves, far away from Nyame and all their spirit friends. Sometimes the boy spirit would wander off and comfort himself by talking to the wind and the trees and then dancing a lonesome dance. But when Iyaloda, the girl spirit, felt sad, she sat and she thought, *and she thought*. At last, one day, she had a really clever thought.

When the boy spirit came back, Iyaloda was excited. She said, all in a rush, "I have had a really clever thought."

"Iyaloda," sighed the boy spirit. "I don't want to hear it.

Your clever thoughts always lead to trouble. Remember the last one . . . '*Let's creep up into Nyame's mouth.*' That's how we got sneezed down here!"

"This is a sensible thought," said Iyaloda. "Listen, we could make some little ones, like us. We could call them children. Then we wouldn't be lonely any more."

"And how could we do that?" asked the boy spirit.

"We could dig out some clay and make little models that look like us and bake them in a fire. Then we could breathe life into them."

"I suppose," said the boy spirit slowly, "I suppose it wouldn't do any harm to try. . . ."

"Let's start making them now," said Iyaloda.

So they dug out clay and made models of little boy children and little girl children, rather like themselves. Then they built a big pile of wood around the models and set it alight.

But Iyaloda was impatient, and it wasn't long before she said, "They must be ready now. Let's look!" And she covered the fire with big green leaves to dampen it down.

When everything was cool, she took out the clay models. Some were pale white, some were pinkish white, and some were creamy white. Each one a little different.

"Oh, they *are* beautiful!" said Iyaloda. "Let's make some more!" So the next day they dug more clay, made more models, built a fire, and set it alight.

"This time," said Iyaloda, "I shall bake them for a good while longer and see what happens."

She waited and she waited, and that was something Iyaloda found hard to do. But at last she decided the models had had a long enough bake, and she covered the fire with leaves.

When everything was cool, she took out the models. This time some were deep black, some were rich dark brown, and some were reddish brown. Each one a little different.

"Oh, they *are* beautiful!" said Iyaloda. "Let's make some more!" So the next day they made more models and set the fire alight again.

"This time," said Iyaloda, "I won't give them a short bake or a long bake. They shall have an in-between bake!"

She waited, and as soon as she thought the models had been baked for an in-between time, she covered the fire with leaves.

And when she took out these models, some were golden yellow and some were golden brown. Each one a little different.

"Oh, they *are* beautiful!" said Iyaloda. "Let's make . . ."

"No!" said the boy spirit. "We have enough children already! The time has come to breathe life into them."

Then they knelt down and breathed into each one in turn, and each little clay model came to life, like children waking from a long sleep. So the boy spirit and Iyaloda, the girl spirit, became the first father and the first mother and, because they had their big family to look after and love, they never again felt lonely.

And, of course, from those first children came all the children of the world, in all their different and beautiful colors.

An African story from the Akan-Ashanti in Ghana

Catch it and Run!

A long, long time ago, all fire belonged to three Fire Beings who kept it hidden in their tepee, high on a mountaintop. They would not share the fire with anyone and guarded it carefully, night and day.

So, when winter came and the fierce winds howled and snow covered the earth, men, women, and children had no way of warming themselves. No fire. No hot food. Nothing at all.

Now Coyote, who is wise, knew about fire, and one year, at winter's end, when he saw how cold and miserable the people were, he decided to steal some fire and give it to them. But how would he do it?

Coyote thought hard.

He called a meeting of the animals, and he said, "Who

will help me steal some fire and give it to the people?"
And Bear, Deer, Squirrel, Chipmunk, and Frog offered
to help.

Coyote thought again.

"Bear," he said, "you are big and strong, so you must
come with me to the Fire Beings' tepee. Deer, Squirrel, and
Chipmunk, you are fast runners, so you must wait beside
the trail, ready to run."

"What about me?" asked Frog. "I'd like to help!"

"Fro-og," sighed Coyote, shaking his head, "you're such
a squatty little thing. You can jump and swim.
But you can't run. There's nothing you can do."

"I could wait by the pond and be ready,"
said Frog. "Just in case . . ."

"You do that," said Coyote. "Wait
and be ready. Just in case . . ."

That made Frog happy. He squatted
down by the pond, and he waited while
the others set off along the trail through
the forest that led to the Fire Beings' mountaintop.

On the way Coyote stopped from time to time and told
one of the animals to wait beside the trail. First Squirrel,
next Chipmunk, and then Deer were left behind, and at last
Bear and Coyote walked on alone.

When they reached the tepee on top of the mountain,
Coyote told Bear to wait in the shadows until he heard
Coyote call "*Aooo!*" Then Bear must make a big, loud rumpus.

Coyote crept up to the tepee. He gave a soft bark, and one of the Fire Beings opened the flap and looked out.

Coyote sort of trembled and said in his quietest, most polite voice, "My legs are freezing cold. May I please put them inside your warm tepee?"

He was so exceedingly polite that the Fire Being said, "Ye-es, all right . . ."

Coyote stepped in his front legs, then he stepped in his back legs, and then he whisked in his tail. He looked longingly at the great blazing fire in the center of the tepee, but he said nothing. He just lay down and closed his eyes as if he were going to sleep. But the next moment he gave a long Coyote call, "*Aooo-ooo!*"

From outside the tepee came the sound of a big, loud rumpus as Bear growled and stamped about.

The Fire Beings all rushed out shouting, "Who's that?" And when they saw Bear, they chased him.

Coyote was ready. He grabbed a piece of burning wood between his teeth and away he ran, out of the tepee and down the mountain.

As soon as the Fire Beings saw Coyote with the firebrand, they abandoned Bear and chased Coyote.

Coyote ran and ran. He was fast, but the Fire Beings were faster, and they came closer.

Then Coyote saw Deer. "Catch it and *run!*" he called and threw the firebrand.

Deer caught it and ran. But he ran so fast that the wind fanned the fire out behind him, and a flame jumped onto his long tail and burned most of it. So that's why Deer has a shortish tail, even today.

Deer was fast, but the Fire Beings were faster, and they came closer.

Then Deer saw Chipmunk. "Catch it and *run!*" he called and threw the firebrand.

Chipmunk caught it and ran. But the Fire Beings came closer and closer, until one of them reached out an arm and clawed his back and left three long black stripes. And that's why Chipmunk has stripes on his back, even today.

Then Chipmunk saw Squirrel. "Catch it and *run!*" he called and threw the firebrand.

Squirrel caught it and ran. But the firebrand had been burning fast and it was now so short that its great heat made Squirrel's bushy tail curl up over his back. And

that's why Squirrel has a curled-up tail, even today.

Squirrel came to the pond. The Fire Beings were right at his back. What could he do?

Then he saw small, squatty Frog, waiting and ready. Just in case . . .

"Catch it and *jump*!" called Squirrel and threw the firebrand, which was now quite tiny.

Frog caught the firebrand, but as he jumped one of the Fire Beings grabbed his tail and pulled it off. And that's why Frog has no tail, even today.

Now when Frog jumped, he landed in the pond, and to save the flames from the water, he gulped down the tiny firebrand. He held his breath, and he swam over to the other side of the pond.

Then Frog saw a tree. "Catch it and *hide*!" he called and coughed up all that was left of the firebrand, just a few bright flames.

And the tree caught the fire and hid it.

The Fire Beings ran around the pond, and they looked for the fire. But it was hidden in the tree, and they didn't know how to get it out again, so they returned to their home, high on the mountaintop.

But Coyote, who is wise, knew how to get fire out of the tree. He knew how to rub two dry sticks together to make a spark that could be fed with pine needles and pine cones and grow into a fire. It was Coyote who taught the people how to do this so that they need not be cold, ever again, in wintertime. And it was Coyote who went around and gave some fire to all the other trees, so that fire lies hidden in every tree, even today.

A Native American tale told by the Karok Indians
of California and the Klamath of Oregon

Maui and his Thousand Tricks

When the world was young, the sun used to race across the sky so fast that the days were very short and the nights were very long.

There was never enough daylight for anyone to finish their work properly, and the children—*well!* they never ever managed to finish their games.

Everybody grumbled. Every day. *Grumble, grumble, grumble.* But there was nothing they could do to make the days longer.

And then Maui was born. He grew up. He became a man. He was Maui, the hero. The great Maui who knew a thousand tricks.

It happened that early one morning Maui and his five brothers set out in their boat to do some fishing. But they had only just dropped their hooks into the water when the sun plunged straight down into the sea, and suddenly it was dark.

Maui was angry. "We must stop that sun racing across the sky," he said. "Yes, you and I, my brothers, must catch her and make her move slowly so that the days are longer."

"Maui," said his brothers, "oh, Maui, no one can catch the sun. No one."

"We shall make a noose," said Maui. "A big strong noose. And we shall catch her."

Truly, Maui knew a thousand tricks, and the next morning he taught his brothers how to twist coconut fiber together and make strong ropes. Then he showed them how to weave the ropes into a big noose with six long ropes attached around the edge—one long rope for each brother.

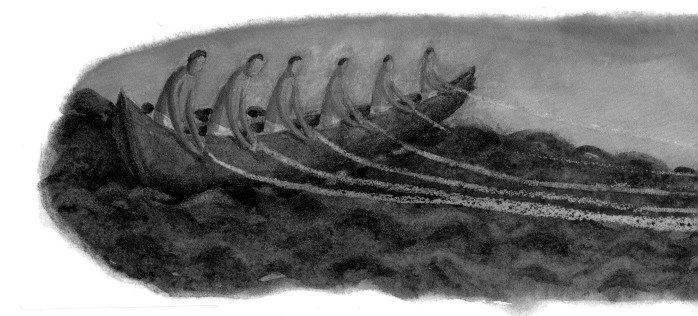

When night came, and the sun couldn't see them, Maui and his brothers took the noose, climbed into their boat, and sailed eastwards. They sailed and sailed until they came to the pit at the edge of the ocean where the sun comes up.

The five brothers were afraid, but Maui chanted, "Hold your rope! Hold it firm! And now, together, *throw!*"

Then they flung the noose over the top of the pit, and each brother held his rope, and together they waited.

Suddenly the sun shot up out of the pit and into the noose and—*whoom!* the ropes broke. They were not strong enough against the power of the sun.

"Ahhh!" cried the five brothers. "What did we tell you? No one can catch the sun!"

"We shall try again," said Maui.

They sailed home, and the next morning Maui told his brothers to collect all the coconut fiber on the island. So they collected every little bit of fiber they could find.

They twisted it into ropes, and then Maui taught them how to plait three strong ropes together to make an exceedingly strong rope. Then, with the plaited ropes, they made another noose.

When night came, Maui and his brothers took this noose and sailed to the pit at the eastern edge of the ocean. They set the noose over the top of the pit. Each brother held his rope, and together they waited.

Once again the sun suddenly shot up out of the pit and into the noose. The brothers held their ropes tight, and the sun pulled and pulled. The ropes were exceedingly strong, but then—*ssszzzzz!* the sun's fierce heat frizzled up the ropes, and she was free.

"Ahhh!" cried the five brothers. "What did we tell you? No one can catch the sun!"

"We shall try again," said Maui.

They sailed home, and on the way Maui thought of his sister, his one and only sister, the beautiful Hina. He knew exactly what he must do, but it made him sad.

The next morning he went to see his sister, who had the most wonderful long black hair that reached right down her back. "Beautiful Hina," said Maui, "will you cut off your hair and give it to me?"

"Cut off my long black hair!" exclaimed Hina. "Why should I do that?"

"There is power in your hair," answered Maui. "With it, I can catch the sun and make her travel slowly across the sky."

"For this alone, I will cut off my hair," said Hina. And she cut off her wonderful long black hair and gave it to Maui.

Then Maui and his brothers wove a noose with their sister's hair. It was fine and light and looked fragile, yet it was wonderfully strong.

When night came, Maui and his brothers took the noose and sailed to the pit at the eastern edge of the ocean, set the noose over the pit, and waited.

Once again the sun suddenly shot up out of the pit and into the noose. The brothers held their ropes tight, and the sun pulled and pulled. The brothers held, held, held, and the sun pulled, pulled, pulled. There was a long struggle, but the ropes made from Hina's wonderful hair did not break, and the sun's fierce heat could not burn them. So the sun, at last, was caught.

"Let me go!" cried the sun. "Set me free!"

"You must first make a promise," said Maui.

"What sort of promise?" asked the sun.

"You must promise to rise *slowly* each morning, and to travel *slowly, very slowly* across the sky, and then to sink *slowly* into the ocean each night, so that the days are always long enough for everyone to finish their work."

"I give my promise," said the sun.

Then Maui and his brothers let go of their ropes and the sun went on her way *slowly, very slowly* with the fine noose still wrapped around her and the fine ropes trailing out behind.

And the ropes made from Hina's wonderful hair still hang from the sun. Anyone who looks carefully toward the sun, when she rises at dawn or sinks into the ocean at sunset, can see them stretched out across the shining water.

When Maui, the hero, and his brothers returned home, everyone was full of happiness. They could see for themselves that the sun was now traveling slowly, and they were thankful. And, from that time on, the days were longer and the people had enough daylight time to finish their work, *and* some left over to rest and play. But the children—*well!* it seems they never ever had quite enough time to finish their games. They always wanted *just a little longer!*

A Polynesian story told in Manihiki

Tortoise's Big Idea

In the begining, nothing ever died. The tortoise and his wife, the man and the woman, the stones—everything there is—lived forever. It was the Maker who arranged it that way.

But one day the tortoise said to his wife, "I've been thinking. What I'd like most of all is to have lots of little tortoises."

"So would I," said his wife. "That would make me very happy. Let's go and ask the Maker for some."

Off went the tortoise and his wife, *crawl, crawl*. They came to where the Maker lived, and they said to him, "Please give us some little tortoises."

"*Mmmm* . . . what you want is children," said the Maker. "Think carefully. If you have children, you can't live forever.

34

A time will come when you must die. Otherwise, there will be too many tortoises."

And the tortoise and his wife said, "First give us children. Then let us die."

"That is how it shall be," said the Maker.

Then the tortoise and his wife went home, *crawl, crawl.* And soon—*great joy! such great joy!* There they were—lots of little tortoise children.

When the man saw all the little tortoise children toddling around, playing with their parents and having fun, he said to the woman, "I too would like to have children."

"So would I," said the woman. "That would make me very happy. Let's go and ask the Maker for some."

Off went the man and the woman, *big strides, big strides*. They came to where the Maker lived, and they said to him, "Please give us some children."

"Are you sure?" said the Maker. "Think carefully. If you have children, you can't live forever. A time will come when you must die. Otherwise, there will be too many men and women."

And the man and the woman said, "First give us children. Then let us die."

"That is how it shall be," said the Maker.

Then the man and the woman went home, *big strides, big strides*. And soon—*great joy! such great joy!* There they were— lots of little children.

The stones saw the tortoise children and human children toddling around, playing with their parents, and having fun. But the stones didn't want to have any children. They were happy as they were. So they didn't go to the Maker.

And even now a time always comes when men, women, and tortoises must die. The Maker arranged it that way, because they have children. But stones, who have no children, they never die. They live forever.

An African story from the Nupe tribe in Nigeria

Raven and the Pea-pod Man

I n distant time, mighty Raven lived in the beautiful Sky Land. He was a bird, big and glossy black, the same as ravens are today. But there was strong magic in his wings and, besides that, he was able to push his beak up to his forehead. Then he became Raven-Man, all cloaked in black feathers and with a raven mask on top of his head.

Once Raven was doing some making, and he made a ball. He waved his wings four times, and—*strong magic!*—it became the sun in the sky. Then, for the first time, it was light in the world here below and, because the sun stayed in the same place and never stopped shining, there was no night.

Raven looked down, and he saw a bare, gray earth plain and empty sea. Nothing more. "What a dull place!" he said. "I must put that right!"

So Raven came flying. But when he landed, he found the earth plain was soft and soggy, like a big mud jelly. He didn't like it. "Here's something else to put right," he said.

He waved his wings four times, and again—*strong magic!*—the mud jelly slowly dried out and hardened until there were only a few soft, muddy places left. At the same time rivers grew, lakes became, and mountains and hills came rippling upwards.

"Good!" said Raven when everything was finished. "Now I must make this dull place beautiful."

Then he flew across the land, swooping and swerving, circling and gliding. From time to time, he waved his wings four times and—*what then?* All kinds of wonderful plants sprang up—moss, fine grasses, delicate flowers, bushes hung with berries, cottonwood trees, clumps of birch, and forests of spruce. And, at last, everywhere was bright and beautiful.

Now one of the plants Raven had made was a wild pea. In four days the plant flowered, and a pea pod grew and grew until it was a very large, plump pea pod. All of a sudden, the very large, plump pea pod burst open and . . . *out jumped a little man!* The moment his feet touched the ground, he grew and grew until he was a full-size man. He waved his arms, shook his hands, and curled his fingers. He lifted one leg, he lifted the other, and walked.

Just then, Raven came flying by. He was surprised when he saw the man. "Who are you?" he asked. "And where did you come from?"

"I came out of the pea pod," said the man.

Raven shook his head. "I made that pea plant," he said. "But I didn't know something like you would come out of it. Still, now you are here, I must teach you how to live."

So Raven began his teaching. First, he showed the man water and told him to drink it. Next, Raven showed him the bushes that had berries that were good to eat. The man liked the berries so much, especially the raspberries and blue-berries, that he smacked his lips loudly when he tasted them.

But Raven was worried. He tipped his head to one side and studied the man. "You're very big," said Raven. "A few berries won't fill your stomach. I must do some more making."

Then Raven led the man down to a small creek where there was some clay. With one wing, Raven pushed his beak, like a mask, up to his forehead, and he became Raven-Man. He took some clay and shaped it into two small models of mountain sheep. He pulled down his beak, became a bird, and waved his wings four times over the models, and . . . *they grew, came to life and bounded away!*

"Oh!" cried the man excitedly. "I must catch them!" And he chased after the sheep.

"Come back!" ordered Raven. "I have not finished my making."

So the man came back.

"Listen," said Raven. "You may catch sheep and kill and eat them. *But don't be greedy!* Only take what you need."

In the same way, Raven shaped more animals. He always made two at a time, and when he brought them to life, he taught the man about them. Raven made the caribou that is good to eat and the muskrat whose sleek fur can make warm clothes. He made the beaver so the man could watch and learn how to make a strong house of wood and mud, and he made the sharp-eyed mouse, just for playful fun. He made insects and birds, some to eat and some just to make the air lively. Then he filled the rivers with fish and the sea with fish, seals, whales, and walrus—all things that are good to eat.

As Raven made each pair of creatures, the man became more and more excited, clapping his hands and dancing around. Once again Raven tipped his head to one side and studied him. "I think I must make two more animals," he said.

He became Raven-Man and made two clay models. Then, as Raven the bird, he waved his wings and . . . *up sprang two enormous, growling grizzly bears!*

The man trembled. "Ohh!" he gasped. "Ohhh!"

"Good," said Raven. "You are afraid. I wanted you to know what fear is."

It seemed that Raven had finished making. But no. He set to work and made another model. He kept looking at the man as he shaped it, and when he was satisfied, he stuck some fine grass on the back of the head and brought it to life and . . . *there stood a woman!*

"I thought you would be lonely living by yourself," said Raven. "So I have made a woman. Be friends, live together, build a house, and have children."

For a little while longer, Raven stayed with the man and the woman, and he shared with them some of his secret knowledge. He showed them how to make a fire drill and twirl it until it made a spark of fire that could set a bunch of dry grass alight. He showed them how to make bows and arrows, spears, nets, and fish traps. He taught them how to make kayaks that could float lightly on the water and how to roast meat and fish. He taught them everything they knew.

When Raven had finished his teaching, he said, "Now I must return to my home in the sky. So I ask you both, man

and woman, to take care of everything I have made. Don't ever kill or destroy thoughtlessly. Never take more than you need. *Don't be greedy!*"

At last Raven flew back to the beautiful Sky Land. But he did not forget the man and the woman. He often looked down and watched them, and their children, and their children's children. . . .

Time passed, time passed, and Raven married a young Snow Goose, and they had a son, Raven-Boy. And Raven loved his only child with a great love and fussed over him and gave him anything he wanted.

There were now many people living on the earth. Raven looked down. He watched them, and he saw that they had forgotten some of the wisdom he had shared with them. They caught more fish than they needed and left the fish to rot. They were always hunting and killing the caribou, the sheep, the walrus, and the seal, carelessly, thoughtlessly, taking much more than they needed. They were greedy.

"I must stop them," said Raven, "before they destroy all my creatures." And, there and then, he took the sun out of the sky and hid it in a skin bag inside his house.

Then it was dark on the earth, and the people were afraid. For them the sun had always been up above, in the same place, brightly shining. They had never known the darkness of night, when only the moon and stars are in the sky.

It was difficult to hunt for food in the dark, so it was not long before everyone was hungry. Then they made prayers to Raven. They laid out their most precious furs and a few choice pieces of food that were left. "Raven," the people said, "Raven, we are hungry. Our children are hungry. We cannot hunt in this darkness. Send back the sun."

After a while Raven was sorry for the people, and he took the sun out of the skin bag and held it up for a short while so that they could do some hunting and fishing. But not too much. Then he hid the sun again, in the skin bag, and it was dark.

Again the people made prayers to Raven, and again he was sorry for them and held up the sun for a little while, and then hid it. And so it went on. Sometimes Raven held up the sun, and sometimes he kept it hidden.

Now Raven's son, Raven-Boy, liked to play with the shining sun, and his father would let him take it out of the skin bag and roll it around inside the house. But Raven-Boy wanted to take the sun and play with it outside. He asked and asked. But this was the one thing his father would not let him do, because then the sun's light could be seen on earth.

Raven-Boy was used to getting his own way, so—what did he do? One day, when his father was sleeping, he picked up the skin bag, with the sun inside it, and flew out of the door and up into the sky.

Raven woke, and when he saw his son flying off with the bag, he thought Raven-Boy was going to hide the sun and keep it entirely for himself. Raven called out, "Raven-Boy, have pity on the people! Do not keep them always in darkness! Sometimes let them see the sun!"

Then Raven-Boy was sorry that he had disobeyed his father. He opened the bag, took out the sun, and put it back in its usual place, up in the sky. He knew his father wanted it sometimes to be dark down on the earth and sometimes light. So then—what did Raven-Boy do? He waved his wings four times, and—*strong magic!*—the sun began to move across the sky and around the earth.

From that time on, there was order on earth. When the sun rose in the east, day began, and when it sank in the west, night came. The people knew when they could hunt and fish, and when they must sleep and rest. And, from that time on, they tried not to kill and destroy carelessly, thoughtlessly. They tried not to take more than they needed. They tried not to be greedy.

So, whenever Raven looked down, he was content.

And Raven-Boy—what happened to him? He did not return to his father's house. Instead he chose a wife, and together they flew down to earth, where they lived and had children.

And Raven-Boy and his wife were the great, great, *very great* grandparents of all the ravens that can be seen today, high in the air, joyfully gliding and circling, tumbling sideways and looping the loop. They have lost their magic powers. Even so, of all birds, the ravens are the wisest. They still have secret knowledge.

An Eskimo story from the Unalit of Alaska

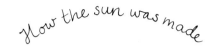

Emu and Eagle's Great Quarrel

In the long-ago Dreamtime, when the world was being made, there was no sun in the sky. The only light came from the moon and stars, so everywhere was always dark and gloomy-gray.

At that time, there were no people. They had not yet been made by Biame, the Great Spirit. But there were lots of birds and animals. They were all much bigger than they are today and much fiercer and more quarrelsome.

Some of the quarrels were caused by the animals and birds bumping into each other in the gloomy-gray darkness. Eagle and Emu's big quarrel, which had such a surprising ending, started like that.

It happened that Eagle was swooping down to catch a little bird for his supper, and, in the gloomy-gray dark, he bumped into Emu, who was strolling along minding his own business. They were both furious. They screamed and screeched, and a fight began. There was a great flurry of feathers as Eagle pecked and clawed, while Emu tried to kick him. Finally Eagle managed to tug out a whole clump of Emu's tail feathers, and Emu gave one of his powerful back kicks and hit Eagle really hard. This made Eagle so angry that he did the most wicked thing he could think of— he flew off to Emu's nest, snatched up a big egg in his claws, and hurled the egg into the air.

Emu's egg flew up and up, right to the sky, and landed on a pile of wood that Biame and his spirit helpers had built. With a great *crack!* the egg broke, and the golden yolk poured out, *and the wood was set alight!* There were just a few tiny flames at first, but they soon grew into a curling, swirling, leaping mass of red and pink and gold. And that was the first bonfire in the sky—*and it lit up the world below.*

The birds and animals were amazed by this new dazzling light. For the first time, they could see things clearly, and instead of feeling quarrelsome, they felt happy and peaceful inside.

Biame and his spirit helpers were amazed, too. For the first time, they were able to see how beautiful the world they were making had become. Then they noticed how happy the birds and animals now were, and that pleased them.

When the fire died down, Biame looked at the gloomy-gray, dark world and he said, "We must make another bonfire in the sky!"

Then he asked his spirit helpers to collect more wood and build another fire and light it. And this was done—and so it has continued. Every time a new fire is lit, it is morning on earth and a new day begins. When the flames blaze up to their hottest and brightest, it is midday; when the fire dies down and the embers glow, it is evening.

Now the birds and animals loved the new bright daytime. But there was one problem. Some of them were such deep sleepers that they didn't wake till it was midday or even later, and they were annoyed at missing so many daylight hours.

Biame thought about this, and he decided to hang a bright star, the morning star, in the eastern sky, just before the fire was lit, to warn everyone that day was coming.

Now the birds were light sleepers, and the star woke them. But most of the animals still went on sleeping. So Biame thought again, and he decided to ask Kookaburra, who had the loudest voice of any bird, to help him.

One of Biame's spirit helpers was sent down to the world in order to find Kookaburra. And it didn't take long. That loud laugh of his—"*Gour-gour-gah-gah!*"—could be heard from a great way off.

"Kookaburra," said the spirit helper, "Biame has work for you. Will you wake every day, when the morning star is first hung in the sky? And then will you laugh your happy laugh and wake everyone?"

"I will!" said Kookaburra. He was very proud to be asked. "Of course I will!"

And Kookaburra kept his promise. Even now he wakes each day, soon after the morning star is hung in the sky. He ruffles his feathers, and he waits. The moment the bonfire in the sky is lit, he opens his big beak, and he laughs— "*Gour-gour-gah-gah!*" And it is such a loud laugh that even the really deep sleepers wake up, ready to enjoy the new day.

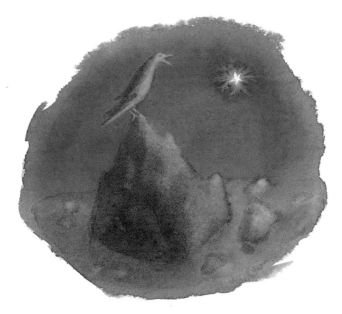

A story told by the Euahlayi tribe of Australian Aborigines

The Magic Millstones

When the world was first made, the water in the sea was fresh and not the least bit salty. And it would be like that today if King Frodi had not been so greedy and unkind.

In the long-ago times, Frodi, King of the Northlands, owned some magic millstones. They looked the same as other millstones that ground up oats or barley. Just two round, heavy stones. It was said, however, that the stones could grind out whatever their owner wished, *if he knew how to make them turn*. But, though the king and his servants tried and tried to move them, the millstones could not be turned.

King Frodi was forever saying, "If only I could turn those millstones, I would grind out so many good things for my people! They would all be happy and peaceful and rich!"

Then one day, two tall, golden-haired women dressed in long, white flowing robes came to see King Frodi. They were powerfully built, like giants, and yet they were splendidly beautiful.

"And what can I do for you?" asked the king.

"Nothing!" answered the two women. "We have come to do something for you! We know how to make the magic millstones turn!"

Then the king was a happy man. "Bring the millstones!" he called to his servants. "Set them up here! Quickly!"

"What shall we grind for you?" asked the two women when the millstones were finally brought in. "Think carefully!"

"Grind peace and happiness for my people," cried the king. "And some gold too."

"These are good wishes," said the two women.

They touched the magic millstones. "Grind, grind! Peace and happiness for the people!" they chanted. "And gold too! Grind on! Grind on!"

From that moment, there was happiness and peace among all the king's people, throughout the land. But King Frodi didn't know about that, because he didn't move out of the room. He just sat there, watching the grains of bright yellow gold pour out from between the stones and pile up on the floor. He had never seen so much gold in one place before—and he wanted more of it, lots more!

After a while, the two women said, "Now it is time for us to rest."

"No!" cried King Frodi. "Keep grinding! Keep grinding!"

So the two women kept on chanting, and the heap of gold grew bigger.

The king could not keep his eyes off it. "I want enough gold to fill the room," he thought. "No, enough to fill the castle. No, the city. Lots and lots of gold."

But as the two women grew tired, they chanted more slowly, and the gold only trickled out. Then the king was angry. "Why did you come to my castle if you did not wish to grind for me?" he said. "Grind faster! Faster!"

Then the two women chanted faster, and the grains of bright yellow gold began to pour out again. All day they kept on chanting and grinding, and all day the king watched.

When evening came, the two women said, "We are very tired. We *must* rest for a while."

But the sight of so much gold had changed the king. "You may rest for as long as it takes to say 'King Frodi!'" he said. "Listen: 'King Frodi!' There, you have rested. Now grind away. Faster! Faster!"

"King Frodi is no longer a good man," said one of the women. "He is greedy and unkind."

"He must be destroyed!" said the other.

Then they chanted, "Grind, grind! Strong, fierce warriors to fight King Frodi. Grind on! Grind on!"

And warriors, all fully armed, leapt out from between the millstones. Ten . . . twenty . . . thirty of them! They surrounded the king, and with their sharp swords they killed him.

But what then? Here was a band of fierce warriors in a country that had been given peace and happiness.

"We can't stay here!" declared the fiercest of the warriors. "Come! Let's take the women and the magic millstones and sail away to another land. Then we shall have everything we want."

So the warriors took the millstones and the two tall, golden-haired women. They boarded a ship and ordered the sailors to set sail, and when the sailors saw the warriors' fierce and awful strength, they had to obey.

When the ship was some distance out at sea, the fiercest warrior said to the two women, "Now turn the millstones and show us what you can do!"

"We are tired," they said. "Let us rest for a while."

"Rest? You shall have no rest! Grind on!" ordered the warrior. "Grind what you like! Salt! Anything! But grind on! Grind on!"

Then the two women touched the millstones. "Grind, grind!" they chanted. "Salt! More salt! Grind on! Grind on!"

And pure white grains of salt poured out from between the stones, until there was a huge pile of salt on the deck.

"That's enough!" cried the fierce warrior. "Quite enough! Stop!"

But the two women only chanted faster and faster, and the salt flowed out over everything and everyone, and the ship began to sink. Even then they went on chanting, faster and faster: "Grind, grind! Salt! More salt! Grind on! Grind on! *And never cease from grinding!*"

And the weight of the salt was so great that the ship sank below the water and down, right down to the bottom of the sea, taking with it the millstones and everyone on board.

Those magic millstones are still lying there at the bottom of the sea, and they are still grinding. So that is why the sea is salt.

An Icelandic story

The Mud on
Turtle's Back

Before our earth became, there was only water, and the birds and animals that swim in it, and the Big Turtle. But, high above, there was a Sky World where the Sky People lived.

One day, the Sky Chief's beautiful daughter was resting in the shade of a tall, flowering tree when there was a loud *brr-oomm!* and the tree fell through a hole in the sky, and the beautiful girl tumbled through the hole after it.

As soon as they heard the noise, the birds and the animals and the Big Turtle looked up—and they saw the tree and the girl falling from the sky.

"Catch her!" called the Big Turtle. "Someone catch her, or she will drown!"

Then, from every direction, animals came swimming and birds came flying. But it was two white swans who flew up and caught the girl on their strong wings and carried her down.

The swans were anxious. "Big Turtle, what shall we do?" they asked. "The girl is heavy. We cannot carry her forever."

"Someone must dive down to the deep places and bring up a little mud," said the Big Turtle. "And then I can make an island."

"I'll go!" said the swift-swimming otter. And down he dived.

But the otter's breath was not big enough, and he could not reach the deep places. So he came back with nothing.

"I'll do it!" said the flat-tailed beaver. And down he dived.

But the beaver's breath was not big enough, and he too could not reach the deep places. So he came back with nothing.

The swans were upset. They didn't know what to do. "Help us!" they cried. "Hurry! Hurry! The girl is heavy! We can't carry her much longer!"

Then an old grandmother toad said very quietly, "Let me try. I might be able to reach the mud." And she took a huge gulp of air, swelled right up, and dived.

Down, down, down she went, and she reached the deep places. She filled her mouth with mud, and she began to swim back. But she was so tired that she swam slower, slower, and *still slower*. When at long last she reached the surface, her strength was almost gone. But somehow she managed to spit the mouthful of mud onto the Big Turtle's back.

And the mud spread and grew, spread and grew, until there was an island on top of the Big Turtle's back. Then the weary swans carried the girl down, and she stepped ashore.

But the mud still spread and grew, until the whole solid earth was made. And to this day the Big Turtle holds the earth on his back, and whenever he moves, the earth quivers and it quakes.

Now the beautiful Sky Chief's daughter, who fell from the sky, gave birth to twin boys who were not alike in any way. One brother was placid, good-natured, and quiet, while the other one was mischievous, noisy, and a troublemaker.

Not long after the birth of her sons, the Sky Chief's daughter died. Then, from her body, three precious, life-giving plants sprang up and grew—the corn, the bean, and the pumpkin vine.

But the twin boys, they were the ones who made the rest of the world, and, because they were so different from one another, the things they made were also entirely different.

The peace-loving brother was the one who made the rich fertile land, sweet fruits and flowering bushes, the dove

and partridge, the buffalo and deer. He made everything that was useful and pleasant.

But the mischievous brother made the swamps and rough, stony places, the bitter fruits and thorny bushes, the wolf, bear, snake, and mosquito. He made everything that caused trouble and pain.

The two brothers didn't agree about anything. They were always quarreling and so, in the end, they agreed to separate. The peace-loving brother stayed in the east, while the mischievous one traveled westwards, making new things on the way. He made the prickly cacti, the hot dry deserts, and the high Rocky Mountains. Those were the sorts of things he made, and to this day they are still there, in the west.

A Native American story told by the Huron

Ra, the Shining Sun God

At the beginning, there was darkness and endless water, and in that water lived the ancient god, Nun, and his only son, Ra. But there was also an underworld, deep down below, and in that underworld was the fierce and enormous snake, Apep.

A time came when Ra decided to leave his father. "I shall be the golden sun," said Ra. Then, shining brightly, like the sun, he slowly rose out of the water.

He was a handsome god, very tall, with the body, legs, and arms of a man and the feathered head of a hawk. And, at all times and everywhere, he shone brightly.

Now when Ra came out of the water, there was nowhere for him to stand. He thought, and a mound of earth appeared. He stood on the mound, and he thought some more.

First he thought of air, and a soft breeze blew. Ra named him the god Shu. Ra thought of moisture, and a light misty cloud floated by. Ra named her the goddess Tefnut.

Next Ra made another god and named him Geb. "You shall be the earth," said Ra. And Geb lay down and became the flat earth. He bent his knees and crooked his elbows, and they became mountains and valleys.

Then Ra made an exceedingly beautiful goddess and named her Nut. "You shall be the sky," said Ra.

And the beautiful Nut arched her body over the earth. Balancing herself on her toes and fingertips, she stretched and stretched, until the great wide arch of the sky became.

When Ra saw how beautiful the goddess Nut was, he made stars and sprinkled them over her, like jewels, so that she would be even more beautiful.

Ra thought again, and he wept big tears, and from each tear sprang a living being—men and women, all the creatures that walk, creep, swim, or fly, and the plants that live among them. Ra wept and wept, until he had made everything that has life.

Then began a time of peace and happiness. Men, women, and children were content, and they worshipped Ra, their shining god, and he ruled over them and was their first Pharaoh. There were never any quarrels or fights. Even the crocodiles hadn't learned how to snap and bite, nor had the snakes learned how to sting.

But after a while the animals forgot the ways of peace and began to attack each other. Men, women, and children too began to quarrel and hurt each other; they forgot about Ra, their shining god, and stopped worshipping him.

Then Ra was sad. "Why do you have to quarrel and fight?" he asked. "Why can't you be friends and live together peacefully?" But the people took no notice of Ra, their shining god, and no one answered.

Ra thought.

"I no longer wish to live in this world," he said. And he rose, up and up, into the sky, where a boat was waiting for him.

He climbed aboard, and off he sailed, across the sky. When he reached the earth's edge, he sailed into the underworld. Then it was dark on earth for the first time. But Ra did not want the people to be afraid. He thought, and he made the moon, so that there would be some soft, silvery light to comfort the people when night came.

Since that time, every day Ra rides in his boat across the blue sky and shines upon the earth. In the evening, he sinks below into the underworld, and there, waiting for him, is that fierce and enormous snake, Apep. Every night Apep coils himself around Ra and his boat and tries to swallow them.

There is always a long struggle, but Ra is *always* the stronger. Each morning, without fail, he returns as a golden disc, shining fresh and bright in the eastern sky. And a new day begins.

An ancient Egyptian story

Feathered Snake and Huracan

At first, there was a noisy god of the sky whose name was Huracan. He was everywhere—in thunder, lightning, wind and rain, darkness and light.

But there was also a quieter god, lying on the calm sea, all hidden under shimmering, blue and green feathers. His name was Feathered Snake.

Somehow, sometime, Huracan and Feathered Snake met and they decided to make the earth. Together they said, "*Earth! Let it be!*"

And the calm sea trembled and bubbled. Big waves rolled across its surface. Land rose up from the depths and rose and rose, until there were high jagged mountains, deep valleys, and wide plains.

Then Huracan and Feathered Snake decided to make living things. Together they said, "*Life! Let it be!*"

And plants sprang up, and the land was filled with color. The sea was filled with fish. The air was filled with birds and insects. Little creatures scurried through the bushes. The pumas and jaguars bounded up the mountains, and the snakes slithered through the grass.

"Now," said Huracan, when everything was made, "the time has come for the birds and animals to thank us for making them."

"You are right!" said Feathered Snake.

Together they said, "*Speak! Call our names! Praise us!*"

But the birds just twittered, whistled, and squawked, while the animals grunted, barked, growled, and roared. Not one of them could speak.

"That wasn't good enough!" said Feathered Snake. He was disappointed. "What shall we do next?"

"We shall make a man," said Huracan.

So they took some mud and shaped it and made the first man. He was the same shape as a man is today. But because the mud was soft he couldn't stand properly, he couldn't speak, and when it rained the water washed him away.

"Again!" said Feathered Snake. "Not good enough! What next?"

"We must make a solid man," said Huracan. "One that doesn't collapse."

So they took some wood and carved it and made a wooden man. He could stand and move and talk. The gods were pleased, and they made some more men, and they made some women too. And the wooden men and women had wooden children.

But the wooden people had no thoughts or feelings. They didn't laugh or cry, and their faces were always blank.

The gods were patient. They waited for a while before Huracan said, "The time has now come for the wooden men and women to thank us for making them."

Together the gods said, "*Speak! Call our names! Praise us!*"

The wooden people heard, but they didn't understand. They didn't know what it meant to be thankful, and they said nothing.

"Yet again!" said Feathered Snake. "Not good enough! What next?"

"I shall destroy them," said Huracan. And he threw down black tarry rain upon the wooden people and drowned most of them. A few of the wooden people, however, managed to escape by running into the forest and climbing trees. They lived on, and their children are still in the trees today. Now they are monkeys—and that is why monkeys look so much like men and women.

Once more the gods met. "I'm not sure," said Feathered

Snake, "whether it's possible to make someone who will be grateful and worship us."

"We must try, once more," answered Huracan. "This time we shall make the man from the seed of the most wonderful plant we have made."

Then they picked some corn cobs. Yellow ones and white ones. They pounded the corn kernels together and added water, and from this mixture they shaped four men.

The men had firm flesh and strong muscles. They stood straight and walked and talked. Besides that, they had feelings. They smiled and frowned, laughed and cried. And they were very clever. When they looked, they could see things that were a long way off. They could even see Huracan and Feathered Snake. They saw everything, and they understood everything. They were like gods.

As soon as they were made, the four men called out, without being asked, "We thank you, Feathered Snake! We thank you, Huracan! You have made us, and we thank you! Twice! Three times, we thank you!"

But what was this? The gods were not pleased.

"These men are *too* good!" said Feathered Snake. "They are perfect! They know everything!"

"If they are like gods, they will not look up to us," said Huracan. "They will be our equals, and before long they will stop praising and worshiping." Huracan thought for a while. "I must dim their eyes," he said.

And he blew a mist into the eyes of the four men, so that they could only see clearly things that were close, and they could no longer understand and explain everything. Then the world seemed full of marvels and mysteries, and so, again and again, the men praised their gods, Feathered Snake and Huracan.

"That's much better!" said Feathered Snake. "Now, have we finished?"

"No," said Huracan. "We must make four women."

They waited until the four men lay down to sleep. Then Huracan and Feathered Snake picked some corn, and made four truly beautiful women, and dimmed their eyes and left them lying asleep beside the four men.

From those four men and four beautiful women came all the people. Their eyes are still dim, and the world to them still seems full of marvels and mysteries—and so they praise their gods, again and again.

A Central American story from the Quiché Maya of Guatemala

Something About the Stories

The Girl who did Some Baking

Different baking time is the reason given as to why people have different colored skin in stories collected from places as far apart as the Philippines, Northern Sudan (Nubian), and North America (Pima Indian). Nyame is the sky god of the Akan-Ashanti of Central Ghana. Retold from J. Bailey, K. McLeish, and D. Spearman, *Gods and Men: Myths and Legends from the World's Religions* (Oxford: Oxford University Press, 1981).

Catch it and Run!

Stealing the first fire from a god or animal who keeps it hidden and is unwilling to share it is a common theme in fire myths throughout the world. This particular animal-relay-race story is widespread among Native Americans. In the western half of the continent, Coyote often does the stealing, while in the east Rabbit is likely to be the thief. I have drawn primarily from versions in: Katharine B. Judson, *Myths and Legends of the Pacific Northwest, especially Washington and Oregon* (Chicago: A. C. McClurg & Co., 1910); Katharine B. Judson, *Myths and Legends of California and the old Southwest* (Chicago: A. C. McClurg & Co., 1912); and Ella Clark, *Indian Legends of the Pacific Northwest* (Berkeley: University of California Press, 1953).

Maui and his Thousand Tricks

Maui is the hero of the Polynesian people, right across the Pacific Ocean. Besides catching the sun, he stole fire, fished up islands, and helped to raise the sky higher. For this retelling, I have drawn mainly from a version collected on Manihiki, which is roughly halfway between Hawaii and New Zealand: Antony Alpers, *Legends of the South Seas* (London: J. Murray, 1970).

Tortoise's Big Idea

In this lovely story from Nigeria (Nupe tribe), the stones, as well as the tortoises and the man and woman, are thought of as having life and spirit: Ulli Beier (ed.), *The Origin of Life and Death: African Creation Myths* (London: Heinemann Educational Books Ltd., 1966). Tortoise is an important character in animal stories told throughout much of the Guinea coast of West Africa.

Raven and the Pea-pod Man

Some elements of this story appear in Eskimo myths collected from Greenland to the Chuckchi Peninsula in Siberia. This myth was told by an old Unalit man from Kigitauik and appears in E. W. Nelson, *The Eskimo About Bering Strait, 18th Annual Report of the Bureau of American Ethnology* (Washington, D.C., 1899). Raven is also the culture-hero of the northwest coast tribes of Native Americans.

Emu and Eagle's Great Quarrel

The Australian Aboriginal creator is a distant figure. Things were made or developed slowly and, sometimes, like the sun in this story, came into being by accident. It is said Aboriginal children mustn't imitate the kookaburra's cry, in case he becomes annoyed and refuses to announce the coming of the day. This tale is from the Euahlayi tribe of southeastern Australia. K. L. Parker, *More Australian Legendary Tales* (London: D. Nutt, 1898).

The Magic Millstones

Two versions of this myth (one in prose, the other a tenth-century poem) were recorded by the great Icelandic scholar, Snorri Sturluson, around 1220, in what is now called the *Prose Edda*. It is possible that as Iceland was colonized from Norway in the ninth century, the story may have originated there. Magic millstones that end up in the sea making salt are also featured in a Norwegian folktale. Interestingly, Saxo Grammaticus, the Danish antiquarian writing in the twelfth century, made a number of references to a legendary King Frodi, whose reign was a golden age of peace and prosperity. Powerful women, like the ones in this story, also appear in Icelandic mythology as Norns, three giantesses who decide one's fate at birth, and as Valkyries who ride unseen into battle, choosing who will live and who will die. John A. MacCulloch, *Mythology of All Races. Vol. 2: Eddic* (Boston: A. Marshall Jones, 1930).

The Mud on Turtle's Back

Some Native Americans call the North American continent "Turtle Island." The story of the girl who fell from the sky is the creation myth of both the Iroquois and Huron groups of Native Americans. The Iroquois, a powerful alliance of six tribes, once dominated an area that stretched from Ontario to North Carolina, and from the Atlantic to Lake Erie. They were often at war with the Huron, a league of four tribes who lived in the Ontario area. In 1648 the Iroquois finally destroyed the Huron villages, and the Huron people were dispersed. My retelling is based on Huron versions in: C. M. Barbeau, *Huron and Wyandot Mythology. Memoir 80, No. 11, Anthropological Series; Department of Mines, Geological Survey* (Ottawa: Government Printing Bureau, 1915). Horatio Hale, *Huron Folklore. Journal of American Folklore, 1888* (Boston: Houghton Mifflin, 1888).

Ra, the Shining Sun God

A number of East African stories tell of Ra's disappointment with people, which caused him to leave the earth. In one tale from Mozambique (Yao tribe), the god Mulungu is upset because the first man and woman burn the grass every day and kill too many of his animals. A spider spins a thread and the god climbs up "on high," where he stays. For background to Egyptian myth see S. G. F. Brandon, *Creation Legends of the Ancient Near East* (London: Hodder & Stoughton, 1963).

Feathered Snake and Huracan

This story appears in the *Popol Vuh*, which is the sacred history of the Quiché Maya who lived in the highlands of western Guatemala. Spanish conquerors destroyed the written records of this ancient civilization, but these were rewritten, in the Latin script, by a member of the tribe during the seventeenth century. This manuscript was lost, but a translation made by a Spanish priest survived. The English version of the *Popol Vuh* which I used was: Delia and Morley Goetz and G. Sylvanus, English trans. from the trans. by Adrián Recinos, *The Popol Vuh* (Norman: University of Oklahoma Press, 1950). The Feathered Snake is also a central character in many of the Aztec/Toltec myths and legends of Mexico. There he was called Quetzalcoatl. Among the Maya of the Yucatan Peninsula, he was known as Kukulcan, while the Quiché Maya named him Gucumatz.